Barbie™ as The Princess and the Pauper

By Mary Man-Kong

From the original screenplay by Cliff Ruby and Elana Lesser

Illustrated by Lisa Falkenstern

Special thanks to Rob Hudnut, Shelley Tabbut, Vicki Jaeger, Monica Lopez, Jesyca C. Durchin, and Mainframe Entertainment

 A GOLDEN BOOK • NEW YORK

Long ago and far away, two lovely little girls were born. Erika grew up in a small village, toiling as a seamstress. Anneliese grew up in a big, beautiful palace, learning her royal duties as a princess. They led very different lives, but they looked exactly the same—except for their hair color.

One day, the queen discovered that the royal gold mines were empty. She wanted her daughter, Anneliese, to marry the rich King Dominick so that there would be enough money to take care of all the people in the kingdom. Princess Anneliese, however, was in love with her tutor, Julian.

"I wish I were free to do what I want," Princess Anneliese said as she and Julian walked through the village.

Suddenly, they heard beautiful singing—it was Erika. The princess saw Erika and thought she was looking in a mirror!

"You look just like me," Princess Anneliese told Erika. "Except for our hair color and this crown-shaped birthmark on my shoulder, we could be twins."

The two girls quickly became friends. The princess learned that Erika had to pay off her parents' debt and worked at Madame Carp's dress shop. Before saying good-bye, Anneliese promised to have Erika sing at the palace one day.

Meanwhile, no one knew that the royal advisor, Pichfingel, had stolen the queen's gold. He was now rich, and he wanted the princess to marry him to save the kingdom. More than anything, he wanted to be king.

When Preminger learned that the princess was going to marry King Dominick, he was furious! He had the princess kidnapped and taken to an abandoned royal cabin. He then told the queen that Princess Anneliese had run away. Preminger hoped that King Dominick would call off the wedding. And the queen would be so grateful when Preminger later returned the princess that she would let him marry her daughter.

Julian didn't believe Preminger's story. He went to Madame Carp's dress shop and asked Erika to help him.

"Me? What can I do?" Erika asked.

"Pretend to be Princess Anneliese while I find out what's going on," said Julian.

"Who would ever believe I'm a princess?" asked Erika.

"Leave that to me," Julian said, smiling.

So with a blond wig and some coaching, Erika learned how to walk, act, and dress like the princess.

Julian went back to the palace and announced that the princess had returned. When King Dominick was introduced to Erika, he fell in love with her beautiful voice and sweet nature. Erika fell in love with the king because he was gentle and kind.

"There's something about you," King Dominick said. "You're honest and down-to-earth. You don't act like a princess."

Erika wished she could tell the king the truth, but first Julian had to find the real princess.

At the royal cabin, Princess Anneliese planned her escape. Covering her cat, Serafina, with a white sheet, the princess called to her kidnappers, "Help! A ghost!"

When Preminger's men rushed to open the door, Serafina dropped the sheet over them. The princess and Serafina then fled to the palace.

Everyone at the palace believed that Erika was the princess—even Preminger. He raced to the cabin to see what had happened to Princess Anneliese. Julian secretly followed him.

Preminger was furious when he discovered that Anneliese was gone.

"Where is the princess, Preminger?" Julian demanded. "What have you done with her?"

"You're the tutor. You should have all the answers," Preminger replied as his men captured Julian.

Princess Anneliese made her way back to the palace gates. But seeing her stained and dirty clothes, no one believed she was the princess. The guards wouldn't let her in! With nowhere else to turn, Anneliese went to Madame Carp's dress shop to see if Erika could help her.

Madame Carp saw the princess and thought she was Erika. "You lazy girl!" the old dressmaker scolded. "You're not leaving until every dress is finished."

Then Madame Carp locked Princess Anneliese in the shop.

The princess tried to send a message to the palace. She tied her royal ring to one of Madame Carp's dress labels and attached it to Serafina's collar.

"Take this to the palace," Princess Anneliese instructed her cat. "When they see the label, it will lead them here."

Unfortunately, Preminger found Serafina first. He went to Madame Carp's shop and pretended that he wanted to help Princess Anneliese. But instead of returning her to the palace, he took the princess to the abandoned gold mine.

When Princess Anneliese found Julian tied up, she realized that Preminger was behind her own kidnapping.

"Now I'm going to tell the queen you've been in an unfortunate mining accident and she'll have to marry me to save the kingdom," Preminger said.

"No one will believe you," said Princess Anneliese.

"They will when they see this!" Preminger laughed as he showed them the princess's ring.

Preminger left the mine and had his men knock down the beams leading to the entrance. Princess Anneliese and Julian were trapped!

At the palace, King Dominick offered Erika a beautiful engagement ring and asked her to marry him.

"But that girl isn't the princess," Preminger announced. "She's an impostor!"

"What proof do you have?" asked King Dominick.

Suddenly, Preminger's dog, Midas, jumped up and pulled off Erika's wig.

"And look at her shoulder," Preminger directed. "There's no royal birthmark. Take her to the dungeon!"

The king's ambassador was outraged. He made the king leave the palace immediately.

Preminger held up Princess Anneliese's royal ring. He told the queen the princess was dead.

"What will I do without my daughter?" cried the queen. "What will become of my kingdom now?"

"I can save your kingdom," said Preminger. "I've made quite a bit of money in my businesses. Marry me and your problem will be solved."

Reluctantly, the queen agreed.

Meanwhile, the princess and Julian were desperately trying to find a way out of the gold mine. Suddenly, Erika's cat, Wolfie, appeared. The clever cat led them toward an old mine shaft, but they couldn't climb to the opening—it was too steep.

As they stopped to rest, Anneliese noticed a rock that had split open, showing sparkling crystals.

"Look! Geodes!" exclaimed the princess. "I never knew we had them in the mine."

Julian swung his pickax and dislodged some of the rocks near a bubbling pool of water. The water shot up like a geyser.

"That's the way out!" shouted Anneliese. The water filled the mine and lifted them through the shaft to freedom.

Meanwhile, Erika sang a beautiful song that slowly put the guards in the dungeon to sleep. She then tiptoed out, right into the arms of—King Dominick! He was dressed as a guard and had returned to rescue her.

"What are you doing here?" Erika asked the king.

"I don't care if you're not the princess," King Dominick said. "I like you for being who you are."

"You're the first person who's ever believed in me," said Erika. As she spoke, she realized that the king was in love with her.

But there was no time to waste—the palace guards would soon realize that Erika was missing. The king and Erika ran to his horse and rode off to safety.

The wedding of Preminger and the queen was about to begin when Princess Anneliese burst in.

"Stop the wedding!" Anneliese shouted.

"It's the impostor!" Preminger exclaimed.

"No, Preminger," the princess said as she showed everyone the crown-shaped birthmark on her shoulder. "I'm Princess Anneliese, and I'm alive!"

Knowing that his evil plan was falling apart, Preminger tried to escape. He jumped onto his horse, Herve, and raced away. But Herve realized that Preminger was evil and galloped right back to the palace. When the horse finally stopped short, Preminger landed in the royal wedding cake and was quickly arrested.

"When I think what might have happened…" The queen shuddered.

"But it didn't, thanks to Erika and Julian," Princess Anneliese said. "Julian is the man I love. He had Erika pretend to be me so he could save me."

"I want you to be happy," the queen told her. "But the kingdom is in trouble."

"Don't worry, Mother. The gold mine isn't worthless after all," the princess explained. "We found geodes in the mines. They're very valuable and will save the kingdom!"

Then the princess thanked Erika and paid off the girl's debt at Madame Carp's shop. Erika was free!

King Dominick proposed to Erika. And after following her dream of singing and traveling the world, she returned to marry the king.

That spring, the most beautiful double wedding the kingdom had ever seen took place. Princess Anneliese married Julian, and Erika married King Dominick. Serafina and Wolfie had many, many kittens together. And they all lived happily ever after.